BRANCHES

BRANCHES

by

Mitch Cullin

illustrated by Ryuzo Kikushima

THE PERMANENT PRESS
SAG HARBOR, NY 11963

Library of Congress Cataloging-in-Publication Data

Cullin, Mitch, 1968-
      Branches / by Mitch Cullin.
          p.   cm.
ISBN 1-57962-061-2
    I.   Title.
    PS3553.U319 B72 2000
    813' .54 - - dc21

                                          99-34827
                                            CIP

First printing: March, 2000

THE PERMANENT PRESS
4170 Noyac Road
Sag Harbor, NY 11963

For Poppy, Sparky, and Vinnie

Thanks to the following for support and inspiration: Brian Bouldrey, Chad, sisters Charise and Chay and the girls, Peter Chang, Barbara Cooper, F & Z, Mary G., Amon Haruta, Bill Hicks, Jemma, godson Jesiah, Kevin, R. K., Martin and Judith, Mom, Miguel P., John N., Bill O., Pete, Renee, Robert P., Clay S., brother Steve, Strummerville--and, of course, Brad Thompson and my father Charles Cullin.

I think I could turn and live with animals, they are so placid

     and self-contain'd,

I stand and look at them long and long.

They do not sweat and whine about their condition,

They do not lie awake in the dark and weep for their sins,

They do not make me sick discussing their duty to God,

Not one is dissatisfied, not one is demented with the mania

     of owning things,

Not one kneels to another, nor to his kind that lived

     thousands of years ago,

Not one is respectable or unhappy over the whole earth.

                 --Walt Whitman, *Song of Myself*

"the old place is nothing"

1.

Somehow

I always end up

right back here,

twenty-two miles

into the heart of isolation:

The old place is nothing

but charred wood now,

all sooty

and cracked timber beams.

The roof is gone.

But the foundation is there,

as if the fire just decided

to take everything

from the waist up,

leaving the rest--

the lumbered floor,

ashen from exposure,

and the rotting support poles

thrust into the gnarled hide

of West Texas--

for the skunks and rattlers

and coyotes to claim.

I don't get out here much anymore.

Truth is,

I stay as far away as possible,

if I can help it.

The two-way chatters

in my patrol car,

little squawks

and bursts of static,

impossible to understand

from where I am

in the yard,

and this dusty,

vagrant wind

doesn't help either.

But that's okay.

What I wish I couldn't hear

is Danny yelling:

Daddy,

I can't move my legs!

I'm sorry,

Daddy!

And I want to shout at him

that I ain't really his daddy,

but he already knows that.

And he's splashing around

like a minnow

down in the well.

I thought the drop

would've killed him,

but I was wrong.

I figured the water

might still be deep enough

to drown the life from him.

But it didn't happen.

And he's not alone down there,

but I don't think he knows it yet.

11

There's two others,

both Mexicans,

probably decomposed to hell

by now.

The stink carries

on up to the yard,

not like any thing

I care to think about--

not like the raunch of shit,

or even spoiled fruit,

as some have mentioned

about decay.

Just Death,

pure and simple,

unmistakable,

the stench of guts

burst open

and bile,

like the last thing in the world

someone would want to smell.

The very last thing

any fella would want

hanging in his nostrils.

Daddy--!

My stepfather said

he built this well,

but I know better.

My stepfather's father told me

he'd built the well.

And I suspect that's the whole truth.

The old man said

he'd gathered all the stones himself--

a month of quarrying around

in this nowhere of nowheres

to find enough rock to line a well.

And it's a dandy too.

What my stepfather did do, though,

was add the little shingled awning,

sheltering the well

like it was a tiny house

13

or oasis or something.

He also put in the draw-pole,

so us kids and my momma

and him too

could crank the bucket

on down down down

to fetch water.

Except the bucket is gone,

so is most of the awning.

So is my stepfather

and my momma.

My older brother Kent,

he's dead too--

skidded his Harley

into a bunch of mesquite trees.

That happened

when I was still working

as a highway patrolman,

and I was first on the scene,

found him tangled in gray limbs,

might as well have been

some tornado-blown scarecrow.

Jesus christ, Kent, I said,

what've you done now?

But he didn't answer

because he was already on his way

to the hereafter.

My younger brother Taft,

he's dead also.

But he died when we was babies

and I don't remember much

about him.

And my older sister Alma,

she lives in Wichita Falls.

And Mr. R.C. Branches,

my natural father,

I never really knew him--

no good tramp of a man,

carrying his tuberculosis retch

to the grave.

So, as far as I know,

I am the last there is

of the Branches men.

Now I'm sitting with my spine

plumb against the well,

sucking on my third Camel.

Everything stretches away

from this spot--

the yard is just weeds

and more weeds,

with chunks of strewn and bent,

rust-absorbed metal bars

from a fallen swingset

poking through the scrub.

I think my legs are broke!

You still there?

Don't go, please!

You still there?

I'm sorry!

And what do I tell my wife?

Danny sobs his head off,

but he ain't flapping around

in the muck no more.

Stupid kid.

Sure enough,

I feel a right asshole

for doing him like this.

It wasn't supposed to happen

this way at all.

But my job

as King County sheriff

is to encourage the law,

and that responsibility

don't stop at my front door.

I loved that boy

as if he were my own,

and almost as much

as I love his momma.

I'm truly heartbroken

at this moment.

And this unforgiving,

sonofabitch breeze

stirring the dirt and leaves,

whistling

through the black frame

of the old house,

might as well be blowing

straight through me.

"this evening it'll most likely rage, consuming the streets of claude"

2.

The wind sweeps

around the well

from a brownish cloud

to the west,

an afternoon zephyr,

a spring gust.

This evening

it'll most likely rage,

consuming the streets

of Claude

with dust

and sand

and throat-swelling air.

When I get home,

I'll dampen a couple of towels,

roll them tight,

wedge them along the bases

of the front and back doors

to stop the filth

from drifting in

through the cracks.

I'll bring the dogs inside.

Mary should have dinner ready

at six.

Tonight is beef burrito night.

It's also

Funniest Home Videos night.

And I'm half starving,

so it'll be three

or four beef burritos

for this fella,

extra cheese

and green chili,

thank you.

Then I'll get reclined

with a Miller Lite.

And Mary will do

whatever it is she does

in the kitchen

after dinner.

And I plan to just laugh

at that program

until my side about pops.

It's just the biggest kick

when those kiddies fall,

or some woman gets bucked

clean from a horse,

or someone leans over a table

to puff out candles

on a birthday cake

and slips face-first

into the white icing.

And I won't explain to Mary

about Danny yet,

because I'll say the boy was going

to his pal Auburn's house

for some sort of homework

get-together.

I'll tell her Danny

told me that.

Tomorrow

I'll organize the search party.

Climbing from my spot

by the well,

I walk to the edge of the yard

to gaze at where the prairie widens

past my boot tips.

Imagine being on some beach

and staring out at an ocean

that floats a zillion chunks

of debris--

tons of scrub brush

and barrel cactuses

and mesquites--

into infinity.

Bits of grime

sprinkle over me,

pricking my cheeks

and forehead.

But I won't shut my eyes

because there's still so much

to take in and wonder at;

the prairieland is alive and wild

in the yellow-orange light,

horndog

with spring fever,

and the widening shadows

of late afternoon.

Taking two steps forward,

it seems that the weirdness

and surprise

of life

are pound into my brain here,

in the asshole of West Texas,

by the whole scattershot nature

of the scrub and critters--

things don't crowd things

as in towns and cities

but are thrown about,

all whompyjawed,

in pasture and peace,

with a huge heaping

of good earth

for each weed

and juniper bramble

and stink beetle,

each plop of cow dung,

so that whatever grows here

sticks out

like a two-foot pecker

at a pissing contest,

fearless

and foolhardy

and brilliant

against the dull soil

and unproductive rock.

I turn,

swinging my shoulders,

popping the stiff vertebrae

between my blades,

and then head back

toward the well.

The painful racket

of Danny weeping

grows louder.

And I cross paths with a giant,

pebbled anthill,

the titty-shaped mound

belonging to red ants;

evil creatures

with grasping pincers

and a nasty sting.

About a five foot radius

around the hill

has been cleared

of dried grass

and other insects.

So I can't help poking my boot

into the belly

of the hive

to stir up trouble.

Put alongside Mexicans,

these red ants

are monsters of intelligence,

hard work,

discipline.

This is truth:

Nothing like TV

and beer

and Mary nearby

to help ease away

a sad day's work.

Nothing like being home

all cozy and relaxed

in the evening

while the world outside

grows filmy and heavy

in swirls of sand;

the faint scratches of grit

against the windows,

the low whistle of the storm

won't be haunting me

one iota.

There's this song

my momma liked to sing--

The oh high lonesome

comes rolling in at night.

The oh high lonesome

shakes the walls with a fright.

The oh high lonesome

scares the dogs and chickens.

The oh high lonesome

shuts the five-and-tens.

That ol' high lonesome

don't bother me none.

Thank you Jesus, thank you Lord

The oh high lonesome is soon gone.

"justice has my grin plastered all over it"

3.

Danny,

does Justice

shoot the bootlegger

holding the baby?

A bootlegger

drunk

on his own tonic.

Bootlegger,

make the brew

in the garage

and swallow it

in the living room

while rocking the baby

in unwashed arms.

But first,

go crazy on hooch

that's just a notch or two

above kerosene.

Tomorrow

go blind from the junk.

But first,

chug a whole mess

to make certain it works.

Then become sloppy

and mean

in temperament

in the living room.

Whip the wife

with the belt

that came wrapped

at Christmas--

black leather,

thick and reliable,

a snake

with a silver-plated

buckle-head.

Beat the wife

until she's a ragdoll.

Take the baby

from the crib.

Watch TV

and sip poison

from a Dixie cup.

Do I shoot this man?

Did I?

A six-month-old baby

squirms

and carries on.

Me:

Let me take you to jail, son.

But don't give up the baby,

bootlegger.

Don't relinquish the child.

Bootlegger:

Try and take this baby

and I'll crush her to death.

Proof in slurred words--

as Sheriff Branches comes closer,

carefully reaching out

with one hand,

the other hand

on the holstered revolver,

squeeze the baby, bootlegger,

and make her scream.

But I'm reasonable.

Not gonna hurt you, friend,

or take your child.

Just come with me.

And child and man

both slip

into the patrol car.

Nobody gets shot.

Even the wife

can walk to the curb,

swearing

between swollen pretty lips,

Fucking lock him away for good!

Get put in jail, bootlegger.

Then pass out.

But first,

rest the baby girl

on a cell bunk.

Then pass out,

so Sheriff Branches

and jailer Riggs

can rescue the child.

Convulse in sleep,

drool and convulse.

Then sleep and dream

about pussy spreading open

like a flower blooming

in slow motion.

Wake up blinder than blind.

Go home three days later,

because Branches knows the score.

Go home blind, bootlegger,

and let the wife be waiting

with Christmas belt

in hand.

Blind fool,

the snap burns

against the thigh,

the buckle-head bites

at the bridge of the nose.

I call that Justice.

Ever fought with a man

who's got a stump arm,

Danny?

Big nigger prick--

Rud Bataan.

Had his left limb

whacked off

right above the wrist.

Sonofabitch

could slip that arm

around a fella's neck

and punch

like a piston firing

with his right fist.

Official report:

Mr. Bataan resisted arrest

while drunk and disorderly

in public.

What'd I do?

Ducked a swing

from that freak,

then pounded the nigger

to the ground.

Bataan, don't try

and find your feet!

Don't kick at me

from the floor

with them clod-hopper shoes!

A lawmen's boots

to the head for Mr. Bataan.

Boot boot boot!

Kicked that asshole

so senseless

his ears came loose.

Know what?

Once I'd dragged him to jail,

had to get Doc Swinsen over

to sew Rud's ears back on.

I've killed plenty, son.

But I've also stepped forward

and spanked guns

from people's hands.

I'm not saying I'm brave.

Perhaps

I just don't have much sense.

Perhaps

I want to treat people

as I'd expect to be treated

in their situation.

I smile and treat folks

as well as I can

and even help them

somehow

before tightening the cuffs.

If I find a person

at his place of business,

let's say Babe's Cafe

or some dive.

I always ask him

to join me outside

for a chat.

See, that's when I put him

under arrest.

And I aim to go overboard

to be kind

to those I apprehend

because it goes back

to a personal standpoint.

Let me explain some

about Justice.

It doesn't go to college,

but works at the family business

instead,

taking up automotive repair

as a sideline.

It fixes old Model T's

and Model A's,

and repairs water pumps,

puts on new fenders,

figures ignition problems.

Justice reaches manhood

with a concrete notion

of right and wrong.

It's partial toward

the due process of the law,

falls in love with men

who are finely dressed,

who stand steady

and unbothered

even in the swelter

of summer,

who fulfill a role in society

in an orderly manner.

Justice now moves

in mysterious ways:

Son,

imagine a dead man's clenched fists

folded across his chest

in some cabin somewhere.

Along the right side of the body

is a double-barrel

hammerless

12-gauge shotgun--

the barrels point

at the head.

A round has struck the face,

tearing away most of it

and cupping back the skull.

Except the fists don't appear

the way they should;

the position is funny.

Slip a finger

to the shotgun's trigger.

Check the safety.

It's *on*.

This means the victim

didn't kill himself.

The official record reflects

that this man died

by a self-inflicted

gunshot wound.

Justice has my grin

plastered all over it.

"his brown gaze showing alertness and smartness"

4.

Danny, listen up.

It's the damnedest thing.

Helen Keller

introduced Akita dogs

to this here United States.

Ain't that something.

Blind,

deaf,

but not dumb.

That woman

knew how to pick'em.

Know what else?

Seeing Mrs. Campbell's

pinto-colored Akita

almost made me bawl

like a little girl.

Beautiful creature

that dog--

bred to hunt deer

and wild pig,

even bears.

A national symbol

in Japan

of good health,

a treasured protector

of the home.

Sweet Pea:

Found dying on her side

in the backyard;

small dark eyes,

with triangular-shaped ears

still erect,

the bushy high-set tail

curled in the grass.

Foul play.

Scraps of alien meat

and bone

suggest poisoning.

Who could've done this, Sheriff?

Who did this?

Four days later--

Tommy Afton's Malamute

called Tiger,

as well as his neighbor

Mike Shaw's Australian Cattle Dog

called Spike

are both suffering

and bleeding

at the mouth.

Again,

alien meat and bone

in the respective yards.

I put Tiger down

with a single shot

between slanting eyes.

Spike isn't that easy.

He scampers

under the porch steps

of Mr. Shaw's house

and yaps with pain.

Three shots are fired,

but only one

hits the mark,

striking the poor beast

in the powerful muzzle.

I pull the wounded dog

out by the collar,

his brown gaze

showing alertness

and smartness,

and pump a final round

into his deep chest.

Mr. Shaw is inconsolable.

Six more dogs

in the month of March--

one Norfolk Terrier

(Baby),

one Basset Hound

(Alfred),

two Chihuahuas

(Pico and Squeaks),

one German Shepherd

(Brutus),

and one Toy Poodle

(MowMow).

Official report:

Death

by potassium cyanide poisoning.

Two weeks ago,

April 1--

Mary brings me coffee

after I shower

and dress

for the day.

Danny listens to his stereo

too loud

in his bedroom.

Someone is killing our dogs.

I go into the backyard

and sit

with my legs crossed.

Who kills dogs anyway?

Roddy Rottweiler sleeps

with his tongue hanging out.

Suzy the Irish Setter

rests a paw on my knee.

Good girl, I say.

Sheriff, she says,

it's Mexicans.

I've figured as much too, Suzy.

Three or four Nationals

were standing outside

Mrs. Campbell's fence

just staring

as I rolled Sweet Pea over

with my boot.

They're everywhere,

watching.

They scattered

when I shot Tiger

and Spike.

At Whitey Fontane's

Exxon Filling Station,

they glance away

when I come strolling in

for a soda pop.

Silent,

nothing faces

under oily baseball caps,

playing dominos.

Mexican boys

and Mexican men

are the same.

They duck in the fields

when I drive past.

They yell in Tex-Mex

when I burst in

on their crap games

or cock fights.

900 square miles

of King County,

407 legal folks reside here

(all but 52 are white),

and I figure the wetbacks

make an additional 100.

The smell of re-fried

comes to mind,

blowing through

the cracked windows

of shotgun shacks.

The stink

of unwashed clothes

and slick bodies

and sneaky hands

in converted garages

that are now illegal Detail Shops.

Sneaky, sneaky hands

pocketing some cyanide tablets

before the poison gets melted

and used to treat

the hard surfaces

of stolen autos.

This is pedigree country.

Mexicans own mutts.

Suzy,

put your head in my lap.

Let me scruffle your low ears.

Let me stroke your long, lean snout.

Your almond-shaped eyes

tell me all I need to know

about Love.

Let my fingers

run through your flat coat,

let them bury

into the longer feathering of fur

on your chest, underbody, legs,

and outstretched tail.

Mexicans, Sheriff.

"come on, branches. come home"

5.

Danny,

I remember sitting here

by this well

as a boy

with the breeze

and the blackness of night

as company.

And I pondered

and entertained

all those serious things--

my teenage urges,

a future beyond Claude,

the color and smell

of worn panties.

I thought

of magical evenings to come,

of owning a Ford,

of hauling ass

over county roads

and highways

to Dairy Marts

and weekend rodeos

and Saturday dances.

I imagined all those wild things

that'd would shape me

in the approaching months.

Sooner or later,

I'd go on inside

and get something to eat

before I headed to bed.

I'd creep

through the dining room,

across the moon shadows

that always fell

on the timbered floor.

Those nights

when I couldn't sleep,

I sprawled on the sheets

in my room

and just listened to crickets

until my body grew heavy,

or until I heard Stepfather's truck

pull into the drive.

I was always ready to pretend

I was sleeping

by the time he returned home

from carousing.

Sometimes

when I knew Stepfather

had closed the door

to his and Momma's room,

I stole outside to this well

and fetched the cold,

fresh water with the bucket.

After slurping my fill,

I usually climbed aboard

the tire swing

that hung from the yard tree,

letting myself float

above the gravel drive,

and spied on Stepfather

through his and Momma's window

as he stripped.

Once his clothes had dropped,

he sometimes stood

at the foot of the bed

near the window,

studying Momma,

who was either asleep,

or faking that she was.

He'd rub between his legs

and scratch at the broad scar

on his inner left thigh,

a long white centipede

slithering toward his balls;

a constant reminder

of a young Japanese soldier

in the Pacific

with a jammed rifle

but a sharp bayonet.

Then he would move

away from the window,

and soon

the bedside lamp

would dim.

My brother Kent

had already gone

to Korea by then.

Sister Alma

had run off

and got married.

It was just me

and Momma,

and Stepfather.

But the bastard

was hardly around.

His time was spent wrangling

in the days,

drinking in the nights,

so usually Momma and I

had the old place and the radio

to ourselves.

Sometimes we danced

to Bobby Folsom's Steel Guitar Band

on *The Old Settler's Reunion Hour*.

Sometimes I lay with Momma

in her and Stepfather's big bed.

Often she'd say,

When you're man enough,

I want you to kill that man.

I want you to get a good job,

take me from here,

and kill that man.

No one knows this, Danny.

Sometimes

I would climb onto the roof

and sit in the nighttime.

Scattered along the black plain,

the glow from oil derricks

shone yellow and white.

Twenty-two miles away,

the phosphorescence

of Claude

burned magenta

under the pitch sky.

I pulled my knees

against my slender chest

as a soft breeze crept

over splintered shingles.

Other nights

I watched

as electricity exploded

across the prairie,

the blinding veins

of lightning

splitting and dying

amongst the clouds.

Rarely did I slumber

more than four or five hours

before breakfast,

but those midnights

of my boyhood

were a pasture that I nurtured

and kept

properly cultivated.

It's sort of crazy,

but I can't seem to set foot

into the burnt out place now.

All that charcoaled wood

and damaged frame

keeps whistling

with the wind, going,

Come on, Branches.

Come home.

But I can't do it, son.

But I'll tell you what,

there's ghosts in there.

I know it.

Two ghosts

just waiting.

One is gripping a fire poker,

the other is slumped

under the rubbish

of the living room.

And I'm the third ghost, Danny,

standing outside

with a gallon of gasoline

and a box of matches.

"if i were the woman, what would i see in me"

6.

A stomach gets restless

this time of day.

Haven't had a bit to munch

since lunch,

and even then

it wasn't much--

fried okra, iced tea,

slice of Millionaire Pie,

and coffee, no cream.

Called home

around 2 or so,

Mary said

she'd have burritos ready

when I got in.

She'd just got done watching

One Life To Live,

and her voice sounded weepy

like it does

when something pitiful

has gone down

in TV-land.

Bring yourself on home early

if you can, she told me.

I'm missing you.

I'm really missing you.

Damn,

if I were the woman,

what would I see in me?

No idea, really.

I'm taller than spit,

and paunchy in the gut.

There's a crease

around my forehead

from this Stetson,

and I've got a farmer's ass,

flat flat flat.

Got a farmer's tan too.

Forearms to my wrists

are tanned brown.

My neck is so burnt

and leathery.

But my pigeon chest

and bird legs

are baby pale.

My eyes are blue,

kind of watery

from this spring pollen.

But I'm hung well,

and Mary knows that.

And she likes that.

In high school,

the other boys

on the football team

called me Rope,

on account

of my pecker length.

Once even won a bet

with this cock of mine.

Ol' cowboy from Guthrie

put six silver dollars

on a tabletop,

said they were mine

if my peter could stretch

from the base of dollar one

to the far edge of dollar six.

So I just whipped myself on out,

plopped God's gift right there

for all to wonder at,

then used my cock

to drag that change

across the table

and into the bowl

of this very hat

on my head.

Sometimes,

while I'm mounting her,

Mary grabs my ass

with both hands,

saying,

There you go, Rope.

That's right,

that's right,

right there.

And tonight,

after dinner,

after *Funniest Home Videos*,

I aim to make love to her

just perfect.

Nothing fancy.

Nothing quick.

I'll put her across the sheets

and take care of business.

Nothing slick or stupid.

Tonight I aim to please.

I plan to bring her knees

over my shoulders

and sort of ease myself

between her

like a middle finger

sinking slowly

into warm butter.
But first,
I'll rub the tip of my pud
against her opening,
sort of tease her that way,
because she just loves
when I'm all playful.
I'll bite her earlobe
and whisper,
Them was the best burritos
you ever made.

I once swore to myself
that no one cooked as good
as my momma.
Then Mary came along
years after Momma passed.
Of course,
she wasn't a girl no more,
had already married
and divorced

that roughneck prick

of a one-eyed bitch

from Amarillo,

but shit could she set my oil

to burning.

She made me things

I ain't ever sampled before

or since--

Apple-Cheese Biscuits,

English Muffin Loaves,

Confetti Hush Puppies,

Blueberry-Banana-Walnut Bread,

Green Chili Corn Bread,

Brown Irish Soda Bread.

It was love, yes sir,

it sure was sweet then.

And it ain't no different now,

except things are more complicated,

a little less sugar-coated.

In September

it was Egg Noodles.

November came

and so did Ham Pasta Primavera.

And somewhere in between

appeared Chicken with Papaya,

and then Coq au Vin--

hard to say,

but sure easy to swallow.

It's been months

since she served Four-Way Chicken

with Ginger-Honey Glaze,

so I expect I've got that

to look forward to soon.

Mary,

I'm thinking,

you're about all I need

to get from one end of the day

to the other.

Sure, you're hair ain't as blond

as it once was,

but give me salt and pepper

over Bananas Foster

any ol' time.

You've grown chubby

around the center now,

my Cream Puff,

my Crepes Suzette.

But when I put my tongue

to your Chocolate Swirl Cheesecake,

when I swish around

in all that soft stuff,

it tastes the same

as always.

Those brown eyes

are still brown,

those wide hips

still buck hard.

Wipe the flour off

on your apron,

rinse them thin hands.

Untie your hair

and let it spread crazy

over your freckled shoulders.

Bring me your burritos,

bring me three,

and later,

dessert

will be on me.

"one skinny milk-white boy"

7.

How does a boy

end up in the well?

How far does he fall?

What makes a boy shave his head

in the winter?

What makes him shave his scalp

clean and shiny smooth?

When did his hair turn

from milk-white to brown?

At what point did this boy

become something more than a boy,

something bigger

and meaner

and quieter?

No more fishing trips to Owl Creek.

No more wrestling in the front yard.

No more sitting outside

with Mom and Stepdad

on spring evenings

to watch the bull bats

sweep above the lawn.

One skinny milk-white boy

with the biggest smile I ever saw

turned sour, pouty,

and muscular

in less than a year.

Was it football?

Was it school?

It sure as hell wasn't girls.

Did Stepdad push him too hard?

Well, did I?

It's a phase, dear.

He'll get past it.

Once he gets girlfriended,

believe me,

he'll settle down some.

The phase:

84

smeared swastikas

in black ink

on spiral notebooks;

odd magazines

coming in the mail--

Blood and Honour,

Mein Kampf America,

Motherland;

the boy with a 9mm Ruger

punching bullet holes

into discarded Sheetrock

in a field

near county road 234.

Sheetrock

cut into six-foot long,

three-foot wide sections

in the garage.

Eight six-foot long,

three-foot wide targets

standing haphazardly

in a pasture

of tall grass.

Eight targets,

each with a different name.

Say them to yourself, boy,

as you shoot shoot shoot.

As you reload

and shoot shoot shoot,

say them under your breath.

Niggers. Faggots. Jews.

Mud races.

Impure races.

FBI. ATF.

Israel.

This ain't the boy

I once joked with

on fishing trips to New Mexico.

He ain't the boy

who put his head in my lap

and slept.

Not this one.

I didn't make this one's bones.

I didn't make him grow.

That boy is dead.

This one will be dead too.

My child is gone,

but he was never mine

to begin with.

That's what I'll tell myself.

That's what I say now.

That's how I'll sleep.

Three years ago,

our lines sank

under deep currents.

Our asses rested

on a wet shore.

He snagged his thumb

on a fishing hook,

and blood spurted

across his freckled face,

burning in his left eye.

I freed that hook

with a quick pull,

and dammit

if he didn't shed a tear.

Then I bandaged his thumb.

Then I dipped my hanky

in the river

and wiped the red

from the bridge of his nose,

his cheek,

his left eyelid.

I put a hand

through his shock of hair.

Later

he caught some rainbow trout,

a whole mess of them fish.

I didn't catch nothing,

except maybe a sense

of what it is

to be a father,

or a dad,

a daddy.

We'd been in Pecos wilderness

for four days.

Last year it changed.

No more fishing.

No more talking.

That boy was gone.

And now this one--

stubble head,

broad chest,

answering questions

with just a dumb shrug

of his shoulders.

In the garage

with his Sheetrock scraps.

In his bedroom

with his Skrewdriver tapes

and red-laced Doc Martens

and thin suspenders.

This one says,

White-power music!

This one dreams

of goose-stepping

in jackboots

on an empty stage

in sweaty boxers,

executing a Nazi salute

in front of cheering skinheads.

As long as homework gets done.

As long as his grades are good.

As long as he's not drinking

with roughnecks and cowboys.

As long as he's making touchdowns.

As long as he's not hurting no one.

As long as he's not killing no one.

Until he finds a girlfriend.

But what's the Jews got to do

with anything

in West Texas?

Nigger problem?

What nigger problem?

Any nigger that makes a problem

ain't in my county long.

Niggers fought in World War II.

My brother Kent

fought the Communists

with niggers and Jews.

What do niggers

and Jews

have to do with anything?

FBI does its job.

ATF does its job.

And no one likes faggots,

not even niggers

and Jews,

I suppose.

Don't got to be a Nazi

to hate faggots

or niggers.

But I don't hate niggers.

I've known quite a few good ones

in my day.

Don't got to be a Nazi

to want mud races

to disappear.

Niggers

and Jews

and faggots

don't kill dogs.

I knew this boy

that made his mother laugh.

He did cartwheels

in the living room.

I knew this boy

with a rainbow-trout smile.

He called me Daddy

because I was the only father

he ever had.

I knew this boy

who gave kisses

to Momma

and Stepdaddy.

He wore blue Snoopy pajamas

and cried easily

when he was sleepy.

I knew that boy.

I loved him,

I guess.

Should've never bought him

that 9mm.

Should've bought him

a dog instead.

"the old place blazed"

8.

Crow haunts that mesquite tree

in the far corner of the yard,

spying on me

since the moment I arrived

with Danny.

Crow eyes--

darker than dark,

like polished coal beads--

squawking out my deeds

to no one,

just the wind,

and the splinter

of dry limbs.

When I was fourteen,

Stepfather made me

take the last long walk

to that mesquite tree, crow.

When a boy practices

his baseball pitch

in the living room

with a Granny Smith apple,

sometimes

he busts cut-crystal steins

on the mantelpiece.

That's how the long walks

sometimes came about--

Told you

not to toss things in the house!

Told you

to keep that dog of yours

out of the kitchen!

Told you

to turn the radio off

when you're done listening!

Pick yourself a switch, son!

Go on now!

Don't make me wait!

And don't cry,

it'll only be worse!

And make sure it's big enough,

or I'll go pick it myself!

Fourteen was the last time

I found a switch for myself.

After that,

I was treated as a man.

Boys get switches

across their backs

and rears.

Men get fists

in the stomach,

slaps to the ears,

heads shoved

into buckets of cold water.

It's easier being a boy,

I think.

But if you're going to beat a boy,

crow, you'd best make sure

you kill him early on,

otherwise the man he'll become

might do you in.

Beat a boy enough times

and he'll turn into a ghost.

He'll spook you

every chance he gets.

So Momma wrapped my ribs

when they got bruised.

And I'd say,

It's okay, Momma.

I drank milk,

made my mouth all slimy,

spit in his soup.

Or she'd rub liniment

on the welts

around my neck.

And I'd say,

It ain't your fault, Momma.

I tinkled on my hand

and twirled my fingers

in his mug of Coors.

Or I'd find her weeping

on her bed,

so I'd say,

Done him good this time, Momma.

Put his toothbrush

up inside me

where the sun don't shine.

And that'd stop her bawling.

We'd get a good laugh

from the secret things

I'd do to Stepfather.

And years after Momma died,

I went once a week

to see Stepfather

at the retirement home

in Matador.

Old fucker couldn't talk then.

Rotting away

from all that drink.

Sitting in a wheelchair,

urinating blood-laced piss

inside his trousers.

Chewing absently

with chunks of chicken fried steak

and gravy

spilling over his lips.

I'd push him all around

in that wobbly chair.

I'd lean near his chin

and whisper,

Branches gonna kill you, Daddy.

Branches gonna sail your ass

in front of a diesel truck.

Branches gonna find a tree switch

and beat you into nothing, old fool.

Know this now, Daddy--

I'm a ghost.

But what I didn't tell him

was that Branches planned to come

into his room one fall evening

after visiting hours

and put a needle in his vein

and inject nothing

but sodium hypochlorite

into his bloodstream.

Wish Momma knew

I'd finally put him away like that,

because she'd have crapped herself

with laughter.

I know it's been said

over and over again,

but it's true, crow,

the last laugh

is the best laugh.

And no sooner had Stepfather gone

into the ground,

when I found myself right here

in this yard,

by this well,

just screaming my brains out

with hilarity.

The old place blazed,

and I just hooted

and slapped my thighs.

It don't matter

that only wetbacks

were living here then.

It don't matter

that I'd grown up here either.

Mexican men

in their underwear and T-shirts

ran through the front door.

Mexican boys and girls

almost naked

followed.

Mexican women

in bras and panties

carried their babies outside.

All of them stood

in the yard

confused,

uncomprehending

my snorting

and hee-hawing

while their home burnt

to a cindered heap--

not even figuring that this

was my home,

not really theirs.

And all that shit burned

and burned and burned,

and I said goodbye to it all.

Goodbye to Stepfather

dragging my dog from the kitchen

and shooting her through the skull.

Goodbye to Momma's tears

and stomach cancer.

Adios

to Stepfather's box of photographs

from the Pacific.

Bye

to the black-and-white shot

of Stepfather squatting proud

and handsome

with his G.I. buddies

smiling all around him;

his left hand pointing a bayonet

at the camera,

his other hand clutching

the black hair

on the severed head

of a Japanese soldier--

the right side of the dead man's face

mangled,

blown away,

a single Asian eyelid

drooping

but not quite concealing

an empty socket.

Goodbye to it all.

Swore I'd never come back, crow.

But I always do.

"children the same as dogs"

9.

Take me far from here.

Oh take me now.

Danny's bellowing

in the well again,

and it's paining my mind.

Just lift me, wind,

send me flying--

a kite cut loose

in the breeze.

Whisk this kite-man

in and out

of a landscape

made of clouds.

Crash me

through a classroom window.

Surprise the teacher

and the kiddies.

Set my body

before a chalk board,

so I may ask,

Who knows how

to get out of a fire?

So all their little hands

go shooting high.

Their mouths want badly

to shout an answer,

but Mrs. Hooper

or Mrs. Christian,

or whoever it is teaching them

when I appear,

has told them to be quiet

and polite.

Be quiet and polite,

I remind them.

You don't want Sheriff Branches

to lock you in jail.

I look for the child

with the biggest eyes.

I look for blue eyes.

What's your name?

She says,

Ann Marie.

I say,

Ann Marie,

tell us how to get out

of a fiery house.

She goes,

On your hands

and knees.

You crawl

on your hands

and knees

so the smoke

won't get you.

I tell her,

That's right.

Very good.

And because she's a Smart Trooper,

I give her a red balloon.

No, I give her two.

I say,

Know what you are, dear?

You're a smart trooper.

I'm as tall as God when I land

in front of their tiny faces.

I rest an elbow on my holster,

scanning their small grins,

their pure expressions.

For twenty years I've done this,

and it's the best part of my job.

I've spoken to first, second,

and third graders

in Claude, Guthrie, Dickens,

and Aspermont.

The teacher introduces me

with something like,

Boys and girls,

today we have

a real life sheriff

here to talk to you

about drugs,

crime,

and safety.

His name is Sheriff Branches,

and I'm sure your parents

have told you

all about him.

Ask them their names.

One by one

they tell me.

Remember them now.

That's Thomas, she's Kim.

He's Mikey, she's Carol.

Hello, Travis.

Hello, Dan.

Aubrey.

Lilah.

Willy.

Who's Tammy?

She's Tammy.

Hello.

You're Robert.

You're Ruth.

I've seen you all before,

many times before.

Children the same as dogs--

eager for attention.

Who am I?

Only hint you'll get--

I'm not really

the kite-man.

Sheriff Branches

with a paper sack of balloons

for Smart Troopers.

Any questions

before I begin my talk?

Well, yes, it's a real gun.

And we don't play with guns,

do we?

Oh, yes,

I've arrested a lot

of bad people.

Well,

sometimes people hurt kids,

but I try to keep that

from happening.

How did I become a sheriff?

Put a finger to my lips

to shush everyone.

Raise my right hand.

Legs straight.

Chest forward.

Say,

I, A.C. Branches,

do solemnly swear

that I will faithfully execute

all lawful precepts directed

to the United States Sheriff,

King County of Texas,

under the authority

of the United States,

make true returns,

take only lawful fees,

and in all things well

and truly,

and without malice

or partiality,

perform the duties of the office

of United States Sheriff,

King County of Texas

during my continuance in office;

and that I will support and defend

the Constitution of the United States

against all enemies,

foreign and domestic;

and I will bear

true faith

and allegiance

to the same;

that I take this obligation

freely,

without any mental reservation

or purpose of evasion;

and that I will well

and faithfully discharge

the duties of the office

upon which I am about to enter:

SO HELP ME GOD!

Red balloons, green balloons.

All colors of balloons

for Smart Troopers.

Take me from here,

put me there.

Make me kite-man.

Lift me from this yard.

Shut the fuck up, Danny,

and die!

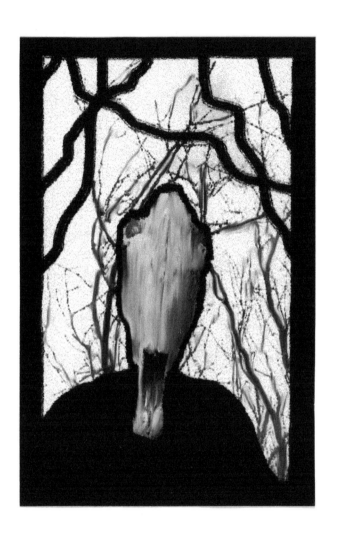

"and i am the son of dogs"

10.

Know what suffering is?

Suffering

is the lovingest

of lovingest eyes

gone hungry

when the bowl is empty.

It's Roddy Rottweiler

urping spit

before he vomits grass

because his stomach

has turned foul,

or Suzy the Irish Setter

dragging herself

across the yard

that time when her stools

turned dark

and unhealthy

and watery

and blood-streaked.

Helpless things suffer.

I'm no vet,

but I'm a dog man.

The Dog Man of Claude,

willing to offer advice

to first-time dog owners.

I say,

Keep your dog on a trolley-line

so it won't stray.

Puppies under six months of age

and sick dogs

should be kept inside.

When your dog barks

too damn much,

hold its muzzle shut

even if it hurts.

Or just surprise the critter

into silence

by dropping a frying pan or tin

on the porch steps.

If your dog jumps on folks,

bring your knee up and bump it

in the belly,

or use your boot

and stomp on its hind paws.

But most of all,

love that pup

to death.

I wrote this poem some time ago:

A dog is your friend,

someone you can depend.

I've had me about four,

and I'll probably have more.

A dog chases cars,

shoots pool in bars.

I've seen dogs playing poker

on this painting by a joker.

I sure like the women,

but dogs keep me grinnin'.

Women are okay,

dogs make my day.

So my dogs will expect scratches

behind the ears

when I get in tonight.

But I'm here

in the swirl of dust

and air.

And Mary is home

waiting.

And I'm tired.

My mouth is dry.

And, to tell the truth,

I'm aching

for the whole mess of creation

and mankind.

And someday

I'll put my holster

and my badge

in this well.

I'll take Mary

and disappear.

There's this stream

in New Mexico

where I plan to fish

until I drop.

There's me on the bank

near this little cabin.

Mary's off cooking

or sewing.

It's evening,

and the pines

sort of shelter everything.

And I'm fishing

with my dogs sleeping

or playing

or watching nearby.

See, there's more to me

than all of this.

I am more

than just Sheriff Branches.

I am not just the badge.

I dream all the time.

Even when I ain't sleeping.

Sometimes

I imagine nothing

but black bleeding black.

There's highways and factories

in my head,

huge industrial refineries

spitting fire

into the night.

Diesel trucks rattle

my sleepless dreams.

Men become circuit breakers

to my thoughts.

But I've read more

than most out here.

Studied *The Bible*.

Walked around for a bit

with Emerson in my pocket.

If a fella thinks I'm stupid,

he's just stupid himself.

I've proven to myself

what it is to be alive

and just here,

but sometimes

it's all so meaningless

I can't stop my brain

from flooding out my ears.

Momma said,

People is messy things.

And the stink of manure,

the filth of heavy bodies

sliding together

behind locked doors

is my take

on this human race.

Stepfather said,

We're all cattle, son.

Don't forget that.

We shit where we eat.

God and Jesus

got a grand sense

of humor.

So don't ask me about God,

because He ain't around.

He's the sonofabitch

that pumps His seed

all over the place

and takes off

when His children

need Him most.

God's got nothing to do

with the two-lanes

and county roads

I police.

God's never been to Texas,

as far as I know.

He's never appeared to me

as a vision,

or made sense of what it is

to wonder about blooming cactuses,

low-hanging clouds

on a fine spring afternoon.

If God came zooming

into town,

I'd throw the bastard in jail.

If He were to put one foot

in my backyard,

I'd burn a hole through Him

so fast

He'd still have a chance

to check His watch

before He hit the ground.

My conclusion:

Man is made

of infinite arrogances,

a multitude of stupidities.

The closest thing

to an honest God there is

is dogs and children alike.

And I am the Son of Dogs.

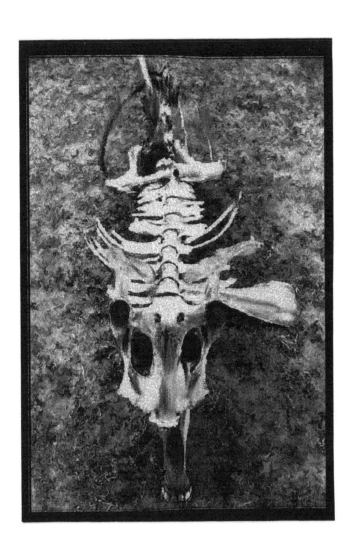

"for every dead dog"

11.

They're nameless to me,

the two bodies

in the well with Danny.

All I know of Mexican men

is shadowed brows

under baseball bills,

following me

from dead dog

to dead dog.

Mexican men behind fences,

poking ginger heads

around the sides

of buildings,

turning to smoke

when I call after them.

Two dead Mexicans now.

But, as hard as it is to admit,

I was wrong.

And Domino Gabriel

knows this.

The only Mexican man I know

by name

is Domino.

A legal National.

The only one I've ever spoken

in a natural manner to.

And he's not easy to miss.

Beer belly,

holding an Orange Crush,

sitting in front of the Court House

with old timers

like himself--

Red Cockburn.

Buddy Merriam.

Bruce Webster.

Three creaky cowboys

with a creakier Mexican.

Domino Gabriel:

fingers fiddling with domino pieces,

spitting brown into Styrofoam,

playing endlessly all day

in the spring

with Red, Buddy, and Bruce

in front of the Court House.

Wrinkled jowls

sucking Red Man.

Broken rim

on that straw hat.

Two men go into the well,

one right after the other,

and Domino stops waving

when I cruise by.

Red, Buddy, and Bruce

raises their hands just a bit,

but all I get

from the oldest Mexican

in King County

is darker than dark eyes

blinking,

135

old crow eyes

telling me

I'm wrong.

Mexicans kill our dogs

sometimes,

because they can't speak English.

How does someone

who can't say the right words

utter discontent?

Poison something then.

Bring hemp or worse

up from Mexico.

Poison children.

Rub cyanide into meat.

Suzy the Irish Setter said,

Mexicans

near the yard last night.

We're next.

And that's how I got it

into my skull.

For every dead dog,

a dead Mexican.

Two men walking

alongside the highway

near a mesquite bramble;

maybe father and son,

maybe brothers,

maybe dog killers

on the prowl.

Mexican men

I ain't seen before,

not that I'd know

if I had.

And they didn't run.

They just stood there

dumb

as I pulled behind them

on the shoulder.

What you two doing out here?

What you got in that backpack, son?

Speak English, boy.

Get over here. Get in here.

You too. Come on.

Been dog hunting?

Know what I'm saying?

Do you understand

what I'm saying?

Can you even understand

what I'm saying to you?

Handcuffed them together,

and both just gibbered Mexican,

playing dumber than normal.

And I guess I knew

what I was going to do,

but they sure didn't.

And if they had,

they sure as fuck

would've flown

into that bramble

when they saw me coming,

and could've got away.

But it didn't happen like that.

And now they're in the well.

How does Domino know?

Wasn't a soul in sight

when I pulled them men

from the car.

Not a thing except this hunk

of fallen house

and that tree

and all that scrub

and grit

going on and on

from where the three of us stood.

Don't remember taking my gun out.

Just remember them two

all nervous,

talking to me in Mexican,

talking to each other in Mexican.

Me nodding,

saying,

You boys been busted

by the wrong end of the law.

No blood spatter,

just teeth

and jaw flying.

A fold of flesh

covering a nose

and upper lip splitting

and flapping over

to show bone.

Horror is the face of the man

who ain't been shot yet,

trying to keep his buddy

on his feet

because the weight

of his sagging friend

is dragging him down too.

Like if he could just get his friend

to stand again

then everything might be fine.

If his dead friend

wasn't handcuffed to him

then he just might be able to escape.

He might not be rotting

where he is today.

"branches, you fool! get after it!"

12.

I've made bad mistakes before.

At least two major goofs

by my count,

and I'm about to pull off my third.

More like regrets, I guess.

But mistakes all the same.

Sometimes

they just land in a fella's lap,

and he gets crazy

and really screws everything up.

Some mistakes come into Claude

driving shiny BMWs.

The first one was on her way

to somewhere else.

Stopped at Babe's Cafe,

sat right across

from yours truly

in a corner booth.

Said,

Sheriff, how far is it

from here to Amarillo?

And I told her.

And she smiled

the widest of smiles,

a half moon shining

just for me.

Mrs. Pretty Young Woman

with Wire Glasses.

Mrs. All Business

with Low-Cut Dress

and Stockinged Knee

Peeking Out

So Perfect.

Mrs. Hello, Sheriff Branches.

Mrs. Worst Mistake

I Ever Made,

dipping slender fingers

into a Country Basket with fries.

And I drank my coffee.

And her eyes

kept talking back to me,

saying,

So you're a real sheriff.

You're the real thing.

And my mouth curved some

as I sipped,

saying,

I'm the real thing all right.

And we didn't have to really speak.

We didn't have to say a word.

And when she left,

I left.

I opened the door for her,

and she slipped on outside.

And I was thinking,

Eyes.

It's always eyes.

Everyone's got eyes,

and that's what they're for--

147

communicating

from the soul.

When a mouth can't talk,

use the eyes.

She drove off,

her BMW calling,

Branches, you fool!

Get after it!

Better do it right this time!

I caught her on Four Mile Hill.

Flashed my lights

and pulled her over.

And she seemed happy

when I came to her door.

She rolled the window on down,

going,

Did I do something?

And I'd read everything wrong.

Because when I leaned

through that window

to kiss her,

she pushed away.

So I grabbed her sweet hair,

and she scratched my face.

All the time my mind is telling her,

This is how you play.

You're playing.

And that's what I said

after I took her from her nice car,

put handcuffs on her soft wrists,

and got her in the backseat

of my cruiser.

And she was screaming

about a million things

I couldn't understand.

Words all whompyjawed to my ears

and garbled.

What she was saying

came out all nonsense

and backasswards

and I told her that.

I put my gun in her mouth

and told her exactly this,

What you're saying is all nuts

and insane,

Mrs. Flirty At Babe's.

But now I figure

I goobered pretty awful,

because I misunderstood all of it.

But what do you do

when you go and do the bad thing?

What happens after you take the gun

from her small mouth?

When you bring that mouth

to your lap?

When she gags

on what's between your legs

and gets your pants all wet

with honeyed dribble?

When you choke her

with what's stiff and stretching

those beautiful red lips apart?

150

When you have to bury her

still breathing in some arroyo bed?

When you slip that BMW

into the deepest,

loneliest,

murkiest watering hole

in King County?

What happens is nothing.

Nothing happens.

No other boot drops.

No one comes searching.

It's like she just went away

from some place

and never came back,

and that's about the spookiest thing

I can imagine a person doing.

It's like she didn't get born anyway,

and that's about how I feel

about her now.

"lawless men hung on the clothes line"

13.

Crow,

the very first gun

that gave me pleasure

was a factory engraved,

gold inlaid,

full blue

Single Action Colt.

Figure I was

about ten-years-old

at the time,

scrappy

and snotty-nosed,

horny as can be

to put a hole in something.

Momma showed me how

to shoot proper.

She took me

behind the house,

held my arm out,

put the gun in my fist,

saying,

Aim low.

That old stump

sitting out there

is a robber.

Sometimes

we'd Crayola villains

after school

or on weekends,

draw nasty grins

and big glowing faces

on torn bedding.

Villains with Stetsons

and pot-bellies.

Crooked Indians

and crookeder niggers

and Mexicans.

Just plain white trash too,

with names like Bart Bandit,

Happy Unlucky,

Dead Man Trigger Finger.

Lawless men

hung on the clothes line

by Momma.

Aim for the gut.

He's comin' for Momma,

you best get him good.

And that Colt rang off

for my unplugged ears.

One. Two. Three.

Four. Five. Six.

Reload. Again.

By sunset

I couldn't hear a damn thing,

but them villains was all holey

and ragged,

just ripped open

and blowing

in the evening,

and ready to be burned

157

with the garbage.

That gun's in my living room now,

locked and encased

in a gray and purple

satin-lined display box.

I've owned and used Colts

since as long as I can remember.

My Stepfather loved Colts too.

Most people do.

And I was no different

than other boys as a kid.

All of us together

on Saturday afternoons

in the Caprock Theater,

our bodies pulsing forward,

excited and shuddering,

at the sight of a six-shooter

blazing from the hip

of Joel McCrea

or Randolph Scott

or Buck Jones

or Hoot Gibson.

No matter how hard I tried

back then,

cap pistols meant little

to my mind.

Call a cap pistol a hogleg

or a plowhandle,

a thumbbuster

or a peacemaker,

it's still a cap pistol.

And cap pistols don't do shit

when it really starts to pour.

When the world goes crazy,

a boy needs an honest gun.

And once that boy has held

a Single Action Army,

once he's oiled it

and cleaned it,

carried it to his room

and slept with it nearby,

all the childhood stuff

of cowboys and Indians

don't add up

to squat.

Danny,

recall how I let you

take the Walther Model PPK

from the shelf.

Your fingers couldn't get enough

of its high polished finish

and black plastic grips.

And I told you then,

and I meant it too,

that someday

I'd give you that gun.

I'm so sorry now.

So sorry.

But god how you enjoyed

cleaning that gun.

And I explained

all you needed to know about it.

I said,

The official name

of the Model PPK

is Honor Weapon

of the Political Leaders.

And you asked all kinds of stuff

about the insignia on the handle,

about the Eagle and swastika

on the left and right side

of the plastic grips

where the Walther Banner

is usually found.

And then you did your homework.

You finally understood

more about that gun

than I ever did.

Then it was me doing the listening

as you said,

The Honor Weapon

of the Political Leader

got awarded

to NSDAP Party members

for doing meritorious service

for the Party.

But I didn't know

what meritorious was,

so I had to look it up--

because I was too embarrassed

to ask you.

And anyway,

I prefer Colts, you know.

That's what I carry with me now.

That's what gets me home at night.

That's what I should've given you,

should've started you on a Colt, son.

"it's getting so brown and dusty i can hardly see past my nose"

14.

Colt Trooper MK III,

my partner of choice.

Caliber: 357 magnum

and 38 special.

Action: Double.

Cylinder: 6-shot,

swing out,

simultaneous ejector.

Sights: Adjustable rear.

Finish: Nickel

with walnut grips.

Weight: About 42 oz.

Estimated Value: $260.00

in excellent condition.

Barrel: 8".

Only dirtied this gun once.

And I've regretted it ever since.

But not a drop of blood

has touched this beauty.

It's my prize, really.

My baby,

and it's borne witness

to my second biggest goof.

As I've said,

more like regrets

than mistakes.

And here we are

together again,

about to bring the day down.

And I'll say this

at this moment,

Gun,

I hope you'll forgive

what I've done,

what I'm about to do too.

I say this before crow

and Danny

and all this nowhere

that used to be my home.

Forgive me.

For I fouled you

in the ass of a man,

and that was wrong.

I put you there

and fucked it all pretty well

and good.

8 inches of barrel

pushing into the slot

of disease and filth,

a seed depository

made of posterior

and intestine.

And how did I make amends?

I put myself in there

afterwards.

Held that cumsucker

by the neck,

bent him

across my desk,

and slammed into him

like a diesel truck

bulldozing a stray cat.

Can't say it felt good.

Can't say it was right

what I did.

If that faggot weren't so scared,

he might've had himself a fine story

to tell his buddies.

How he bagged a man

with a badge,

or how a man

with a badge

bagged him

right in the shitter.

Let him go too,

so he'd blab

to his drug-pushing friends.

So he'd warn them

to keep their pills

and grass

and swishy walks

and funny mustaches

away from Claude.

So he'd mention getting busted

when speeding

in the middle of the night,

drunk,

maybe stoned,

maybe both.

And I treated him fairly nice

at first,

because he was agreeable.

And when I frisked him

there on the shoulder,

he joked that it tickled.

Then he went,

Don't look under the seat,

so I did.

Because only a dumbshit

says something like that.

And jesus christ

suddenly I'm flipping

through these magazines

with naked young men

showing whopping dicks

and butt cracks

and balls shaved clean.

Guess I'm caught, officer.

You sure are, friend.

One plastic bag of amphetamines

in the glove case

means nailed

and jailed

for a long stretch.

But that's not what happened,

because no sooner is he in my office

then I got his shorts

around his knees.

And what am I telling him?

I'm going,

You like it like that?

What do you put up in there

anyway?

That's when he got frightened.

That's when I showed him my gun.

Slid it in and out

of his mouth,

in and out

of his ass,

and, truthfully,

it got me hard as can be doing that.

Once I'd pulled my pecker

from his stinkhole

and shot hot,

thick squirts

all over his cheeks,

my body got drained

and sleepy.

Get out of here!

Don't ever come back,

or I'll kill you, son!

Don't ever come this way again!

Then he was gone

like he hadn't even been there.

Just some idea

I'd made in my head.

Which is how I imagine him

when I imagine him.

So, by all accounts,

that boy should be in the well;

now there's someone

who needs to sink

in death

and stench.

And I'm sad about that, gun,

because I did you bad then.

But I polished you

all smooth that night.

Like I do every night.

And I hurt a lot

about putting myself

inside another man.

But if a fella can count his mistakes

on one hand,

then he's doing okay.

And I'm doing okay.

Mistakes is how we learn, Danny.

We become better men

from our mistakes.

But I suspect

I've said too much.

I've thought too much.

It's getting so brown

and dusty

I can hardly see

past my nose,

and Mary's probably waiting

while those burritos

are warming in the oven.

"a black hole in the middle of west texas"

15.

Rain thumps my hat.

Drops hit my shoulders,

sneaking under my collar,

slipping inside my ear

to whisper,

Time to hit the road, Branches.

Be done

with what's got to be done.

But I've not said

what I must say, Danny.

Because I know it was you now,

and not them Mexicans.

And Domino knows.

And crow knows.

And I'm just glad it was Mexicans

I'd gone and made vanish,

otherwise I'd be more bothered

than I am.

Sniffling won't get you

out of this one, son.

You can't save yourself,

so just sit quiet

down there

and listen while you can.

A young man kills dogs

because he wants to kill something,

I guess.

Kills dogs because he must,

I suppose.

But you left those damn booklets

on your bed.

Pages folded at the top,

bringing me to that article

in *Blood and Honour*,

titled in red and black--

Prepare for the Holocaust.

So I sat there on your bed

just this morning.

Me in your room

with those words yapping:

When the time comes,

brothers and sisters,

it's important to be ready.

Practice breeds diligence

and discipline.

A racial Holy War,

our beloved Rahowa,

is already in the making,

though it may not feel like it

in your neck of the woods.

Don't despair.

What can you do

to prepare yourself?

Gas chambers

won't be easily available

during the first year of Rahowa,

but common household items

that can inflict death

through poisoning

179

will be.

Michael Burmeister

discusses the quick art

of tainting,

providing helpful hints

on how to legally acquire cyanide

and nitric.

He will also detail ways

to make cooking gas

and caustic soda

lethal weapons

against the Jewish conspiracy.

Study and get ready.

Remember,

practice gives you an edge

against the enemy,

and Michael offers suggestions

about who and what

to practice on.

Rain wants me to finish.

Pat pat patting

my back and arms.

The old place is howling, Danny.

My heart is leaking tears.

A storm roars in my gut.

And I'm grateful

that you didn't do Suzy

or Roddy,

but that's about all

I'm grateful for.

Your precious mother,

my Mary,

will be ruined by week's end.

Her only child has left,

and he ain't ever coming home.

But she don't understand this yet.

Her happy boy grew fast

and spoiled into something bad

and strange

and rotten

I can't make sense of,

except she won't recall you like that.

I'll make sure she don't.

I promise.

Gun and crow,

witness my third goof.

Wind and rain

pound my frame

into a gully of regret.

Dust devils

whip the ground,

whisk the russet earth

toward the judging sky.

I'm still with you, Danny.

But the day has slipped

into something dimmer

than night.

Dwell on this for a second, son.

Put yourself in bed as a boy.

Feel my hands pushing the sheets in

182

around your stomach and legs.

Each night until you turned twelve,

I rubbed your palms.

A nightlight shone on Stepdad

stooping to kiss Stepson

on the forehead.

That's a million miles

from where we find ourselves

this evening.

Stepdad taking the slow walk

with Stepson

from the patrol car

to the well.

Look in there, Danny.

What do you see?

How far is it?

Get yourself over the top some

and stare

at what's down there.

A black hole

in the middle

of West Texas,

twisting, burbling, invisible.

What goes in

don't ever come out.

As a child,

during my midnight ambles,

I spied starlight flickering

at the bottom,

caught in the still water.

Reach for the stars

in the well,

but it's too deep

for boys and men.

And stars ain't meant

to be touched anyway, Danny.

Can you spot anything?

Stepdad brings his fingers

to the loops of Stepson's jeans,

gives a fast shove,

sending the Dog Killer

into space.

Son,

my remorse

is as down-reaching

and sunless

as this hole you're in.

And that's the last

of what I got to utter

to you.

"some men are more fearful than the monsters they kill"

16.

Shot one

gets him going again.

Daddy--!

Second shot

knocks the voice from him.

Third shot

ricochets, sparking

along the rock wall.

Number four drowns

all that splashing he's doing.

Five hits the mark.

Six does too.

Reload. Again.

Left hand

on my right wrist.

Gun aimed straight

into the mouth

of the well.

Ears buzzing.

With the nozzle flash and burst,

I steal good glimpses

at hell.

Three bodies floating,

sardine men,

scalps and limbs

submerged.

Shooting fish in a barrel.

And it don't matter no more

which body is Danny.

I just empty

and reload.

Empty and reload.

That's what I do.

Until I can't hear a thing.

Until the only noise there is

is my brain bellowing,

telling me again

and again,

Some days

are better than others.

Some days

are better than others.

And now I'm sitting

once more

with my back to the well.

I'm on my last Camel,

taking comfort

in what's filling my lungs.

Blowing smoke

at a world consumed

with weeds

and lightning

and soft falling rain.

Crow balks

from its place in the yard tree,

screaming to the fallen swingset,

making clear to that zephyr

and shit-spitting cloud

that some men

are more fearful

than the monsters they kill.

Scatter toward the storm, crow,

because if my gun

hadn't spent its last shell,

I'd blow your black-eyed skull

across the old house

and into scrub.

This is what I figure:

Not a man walking

who doesn't live

with his errors.

Once Momma said,

A man's a man

when he can stare

at himself

in the mirror

and don't blink

at what he finds

returning his gaze.

To make right,

a fella has to get muddy

every so often.

He's got to catch hold

of a problem

before it becomes a problem.

He's got to make the sacrifices

others ain't willing to make.

I've made my peace

with myself.

No soul in Claude has to fret

with locking doors

before bedtime.

Dogs and children

slumber easy.

Keys can stay in the ignition

overnight.

I'm doing my job.

My goofs seem slight

when I pause a moment

to put my face

193

in front of that mirror.

I never blink

at what returns my gaze.

Truth is,

sometimes

I don't see nothing there,

and that's okay with me.

Ghosts come and go

as they please.

So I'm done.

This rain ain't about to tire.

Mary's wondering for sure,

and I'm hungry.

And tomorrow

I search for my boy.

I'll start with his friends.

I'll talk to his teachers.

There'll be leads all right,

and I'll follow each one

to the disappointing end.

And there's Domino.

But he can wait.

This well won't be ready

for a month or so,

and I ain't too eager

to get out here soon.

But tonight it's burritos

and *Funniest Home Videos*.

Tonight

the streets of Claude get swept

with grit and sand.

Tomorrow

this sad scene

becomes memory,

and I'll sleep sound.

I'll get the dogs inside,

make sure the storm

don't creep under the doors

and windows.

And I'll drink a couple

of Miller Lites.

Then it's to bed with Mary.

Gun,

better believe Branches

is going to hump

and grind

this pitiful wreck of an evening

into the past.

So let the storm commence.

I'm going home.

This is how I walk away--

yank the brim of my hat

over my brow,

shake the rain

from my shoulders.

Forward

and don't turn around

in case something

might be crawling

past the rim of the well.

Something might be moving

beneath the scraps

of the old place.

The moon is up there

somewhere,

round and full

and glowing.

Just a puffy layer

of brooding clouds

acting selfish

with the stars.

I slip behind the wheel

of the cruiser,

thinking what I like to think

in my mind

while driving home,

Night brings no gloom

to the heart

with its welcome shade.